CHICKEN
MISSION

ORCHARD BOOKS
96 Leonard Street, London EC2A 4RH
Orchard Books Australia
14 Mars Road, Lane Cove, NSW 2066
First published in Great Britain in 1988 as *Meet the Greens*
This edition first published in hardback in 1996
Paperback first published 1997
Text © Sue Limb 1988
Illustrations © Sue Heap 1996
The right of Sue Limb to be identified as the Author
and Sue Heap as the Illustrator of this Work
has been asserted by them in accordance with
the Copyright, Designs and Patents Act, 1988.
A CIP catalogue record for this book is available
from the British Library.
1 86039 270 9 (hardback)
1 86039 081 1 (paperback)
Printed in Great Britain

CHICKEN MISSION
A Lizzie Green story

Sue Limb

Illustrated by
Sue Heap

ORCHARD BOOKS

Lizzie Green stories

Chicken Mission

Tree Trouble

Contents

1

Meet the Greens

"Go and do some shopping for me, please, you two!" said Lizzie's mum. Lizzie's brother Tom groaned. He was very busy lying on the sofa and drinking a can of coke.

"Oh, Mum!" he said. "That Buster Keaton film is on in a minute! Why can't she go on her own?"

"I'm too young," said Lizzie, bouncing off the armchair and running for the shopping basket. "I might get mugged or kidnapped by a desperate man with a black beard."

"Ten minutes with you and his beard would turn grey," said Tom, moving one leg idly off the sofa.

"Oh, come on, Tom," said Mrs Green. "If you want any breakfast tomorrow you'll have to go and get it. Here's the list: bacon, eggs, butter and coffee. I haven't got time to go myself: I've got all these envelopes to address. Get a move on! The shops'll be shut in ten minutes."

Tom and Lizzie's mother worked very hard. In the daytime she was a receptionist at

the local hotel: in the evening, sometimes, she addressed envelopes and delivered things. She ran everywhere, she was always tired, and she never had enough time. She even made sandwiches every morning for Dad, whilst he sat and stared out of the window. Lizzie did not think this was quite fair.

She loved her dad very much, though. Mr Green worked in a garage. He always came home covered in oil.

"Don't touch those envelopes!" Mum would cry. "I don't want oily fingerprints all over them!" And she would run off to the kitchen to get a rag. Lizzie's dad would stand and watch TV, wiping his fingers very slowly on the rag. He did everything very slowly—except drive the car.

"Ah," he'd say, after a while, watching the news. "Turned out nice again."

He always said this if it was raining. Lizzie's dad was a bit of a joker.

"Right," said Tom, swinging his other leg off the sofa and sitting up. He looked at the shopping list.

"Bacon," he said. "Pig's bum. I like a bit of pig's bum. Not while it's still on the pig, of course."

Tom fancied himself as a bit of a joker, too.

"Tom!" said his mother. "I don't like that kind of talk. Now here's the money. Get a move on!"

10

Lizzie didn't like that kind of talk, either. But not for the same reasons. Lizzie was fond of bacon, but she didn't like thinking that it had once been a pig. It seemed a shame, really. Why couldn't bacon grow on trees, like apples and pears and cherries? Then her mum could say, "Lizzie, just run out and pick a bit of bacon for breakfast, will you?"

But Lizzie knew that life wasn't like that.

Eggs were all right, though. Hens lay them and we eat them, thought Lizzie. That seems fair enough. I don't suppose the hens mind, really. They're probably quite pleased.

Tom stood up and zipped the five pound note into his top pocket. This was progress.

"Oh, wait!" said Lizzie, suddenly remembering. "I must bring Kalamazoo!"

"Gordon Bennett! That bear!" grumbled Tom, finishing the last of his coke. Lizzie raced upstairs. There, lying on her bed and looking pale and anxious, was Kalamazoo, her bear pyjama case.

He was an American bear, and very old. He'd been Lizzie's auntie's bear. She had

grown up in America. By now nearly all his fur had gone. One of his original eyes was lost, too. Lizzie's mum had sewed on a brown button in its place. Kalamazoo was very self-conscious about this. He wished his eyes matched. He was also embarrassed about how fat he looked when Lizzie zipped her pyjamas into him. All in all he had a sad kind of look. His smile had dropped off fifteen years ago, which is a pretty terrible thing to happen to anyone.

"It's okay, you can leave me here," he said, as soon as Lizzie came in. "Those awful supermarkets! Everybody'll laugh at me because of my odd eyes. I can't bear it. I'm a sensitive person. And I won't be able to smile at anybody either. Not that I shall feel like smiling. When did I last smile? What do I have to smile about?"

"Oh, come on, Kalamazoo!" said Lizzie firmly. "You know it does you good to get out. It's no use moping around home all day."

"I wouldn't mope!" said Kalamazoo indignantly. "I'm having some very important philosophical thoughts. I shall write a book soon, I expect. Wait! If I must go out, for goodness' sake take these pyjamas out of me. I don't want people to think I'm fat."

"Come on, Lizzie!" yelled Tom up the stairs.

"Is that dreadful boy coming with us?" said Kalamazoo, trembling. "He's such a barbarian!"

Lizzie wasn't sure what barbarian meant, but she was sure Kalamazoo did. He was a very educated bear. He'd been to college in America with Lizzie's auntie. But all that education hadn't done much for his bravery. Even Lizzie had to admit he could be a total wimp at times. She pulled her pyjamas out of

his insides ("Gently!" s c r e a m e d Kalamazoo) and carried him downstairs.

"Ah! I see a pair of bald bear's legs!" said Tom, tweaking Kalamazoo's toe. "A bit past it, ain't he? I should sell him if I were you, Lizzie. These old bears can be worth quite a bit, at an auction. I saw it on telly the other day."

Kalamazoo went even paler, and his fur began to tremble. Lizzie saw this, and understood. She held him very tight.

"I wouldn't sell Kalamazoo for anything, ever!" she said. "He's not just a bear, he's a distinguished personality!"

Kalamazoo stopped trembling. He could take any amount of flattery.

"But you could get enough money for a pair of roller skates!" said Tom. "Maybe even ice skates as well. Maybe even enough money for skating lessons."

"I'm saving up for skates," said Lizzie firmly. "But I wouldn't sell Kalamazoo for all the skating lessons in the world."

"Deeply touching!" said Tom, laughing. "You'll have me crying in a minute."

He knew how much Lizzie dreamed of skating lessons. But Lizzie said nothing. She just held on tight to Kalamazoo's left leg, so he would know he was safe. She was going to enjoy her walk to the shops. There was so much to see.

2

The Dreaded Griffo

There were lots of things about the walk that Lizzie liked. The Greens lived on the edge of town, so there was an odd mixture of towny things and country things: a shop that did picture-framing, all on its own, with tools and bits of frame in the window. This shop was nearly always shut. Then there was the newsagent's, run by Mr and Mrs Patel, which was nearly always open. Mrs Patel kept an eye on the magazines, and if there was anything about skating in them, she showed it to Lizzie. Tom did a paper round for Mr Patel, and he often brought a packet of crisps home for Lizzie – a present from Mrs Patel. So the Patels' shop was a favourite place.

Just past the Patels' was a field where two donkeys lived. They liked crisps too. Then there were some deserted old factories, which looked to Lizzie as if they might be haunted; and some new factories, tucked away amongst some trees; and a plant

nursery where Lizzie always bought her mum's birthday and Christmas presents. Mrs Green liked potted plants, especially ones that smelt nice.

Beyond the plant nursery, Lizzie stopped and wrinkled her nose. Now *this* was a smell that wasn't nice at all.

"Ugh!" said Lizzie. "Why does it always smell so horrible, just here?"

"I thought it was you," said Tom with a teasing grin.

"No, stop it Tom, don't be silly. You know it always smells horrible just here. What is it?"

"It's Dewey's," said Tom, pointing to a big building tucked away behind some trees.

"What's Dewey's?" asked Lizzie. "A glue factory? It smells like it."

"It's a chicken farm, innit, stupid!" said Tom. "Haven't you seen their adverts? DIVE INTO A DEWEY'S EGG – FRESH AS THE DEW."

"But it can't be a farm, Tom," said Lizzie. She knew what farms were like. She'd seen pictures of them in her books. "If it was a farm," she went on, "the hens would all be wandering round the farmyard, outside, wouldn't they?"

"Shows how much you know," said Tom scornfully. "I know a bloke who works there, see?"

"Who?"

"Griffo."

Lizzie felt scared. She'd always been a bit frightened of Paul Griffin. He was tall and wore a tattered coat and he had a strange, wild look about him. But even as she thought these things, there was the screech of bike tyres and there was Griffo, right behind them.

"Out of my way, Green," said Griffo. "This

your little sister, innit, Tom?"

"Yeah. She doesn't believe there are chickens in there," said Tom, nodding towards the big building. "She thinks that hens walk about out of doors."

"Behind the times, you are, sweetheart," said Griffo.

"Do you mean, there really are hens in there?" asked Lizzie timidly, holding on tight to Kalamazoo. "But don't they make a mess on the floor, and everything?"

Griffo threw back his head and laughed. It was a nasty laugh, and Lizzie could see his teeth, something she'd rather have done without.

"They don't walk about," said Griffo, after he'd got tired of laughing. "They're all in cages, see? Five to a cage. Much as they can do to sneeze, let alone go on sponsored walks."

"Five to a box?" said Lizzie. "That sounds a bit crowded."

"Oh, no, darlin'. It's all scientific."

"What?" asked Lizzie.

"Scientific, stupid," said Tom. "The way they're kept. Not like in the bad old days."

"What do you do then, Griffo?" asked Lizzie.

"Oh, I feed them...put drugs in their food, if they need it. Knock out drops if they're getting uppity."

And Griffo laughed again. A most unpleasant laugh.

"And I suppose you let them out for exercise?" said Lizzie.

"Exercise?" hooted Griffo. "They don't get any. They're not racehorses!"

"Stupid!" said Tom. But Lizzie didn't care. She simply didn't believe that hens could live in cages all day and all night.

"I don't believe you!" she said. "I couldn't  live in a cage all the time."

"They're not like us," said Tom. "They don't mind."

"If you don't believe me," said Griffo, "come and see for yourself."

"All right!" said Lizzie, suddenly very brave. "When?"

"Tomorrow!" said Griffo. "Be here at ten. I've got the keys and everything. I'm Dewey's right-hand man."

And he cycled off, whistling, looking very important and pleased with himself.

Lizzie didn't feel so pleased, though. Maybe she would stay at home tomorrow. She didn't like Griffo and she didn't like what he'd said about Dewey's.

"You've done it now," said Tom. "I expect he'll strangle you and feed you to the hens. He's totally mad, you know."

"Ah well," said Lizzie, trying to sound calm, "that makes two of you, doesn't it?"

And she marched off to the shops.

3

Eggs for Supper

At the supermarket, Lizzie went in to do the shopping while Tom waited outside. It was beneath his dignity to go round with the trolley and besides, he was hoping for a glimpse of Caroline Elliott. Lizzie knew this but was too tactful to mention it. Judging by the way Tom scowled and punched the walls, he was feeling very nervous indeed. Lizzie felt sorry for boys. Having to do all that scowling and kicking kerbstones and punching walls must be a real drag. Whereas girls could just get on with enjoying life.

"I'm going to get travel sick on this trolley," said Kalamazoo as they whizzed past the yoghurts. "You know I have a delicate stomach. For goodness' sake! Slow down!"

Lizzie wasn't really listening though. She was looking for the eggs. There they were. DEWEY'S EGGS it said on the box. FRESH AS THE DEW. And on the  side it said COUNTRY FARM FRESH. Lizzie couldn't believe these eggs had come out of that strange building with no windows. How could they possibly call them country farm fresh? Dewey's wasn't a country farm, at all. It looked more like a factory.

"You know what I think, Kalamazoo," said Lizzie, as she put a box of eggs in her trolley, " I think Tom and Griffo are kidding me."

"Well, you'll find out tomorrow," said Kalamazoo. "Too bad I can't come with you. I have an important meeting."

"You've got to come with me, Kalamazoo!" said Lizzie. "You're my minder. You'll keep me safe."

"Sorry," said Kalamazoo, "I just can't make it. I've got, er – other things I must do."

"Oh, yes? Like what?" demanded Lizzie.

"I am giving a little talk to the other toys," said Kalamazoo with dignity. "It's called *The Importance of the Teddy Bear in History.*"

"Crumbs!" said Lizzie. "I bet they'll all be relieved when you tell them you have to cancel it." And she got up a bit of speed as she neared the checkout.

"Slow this trolley down!" screamed Kalamazoo. "I'll come with you tomorrow! Anything!"

Lizzie slowed down. She paid for the shopping and went out to where Tom was waiting. He looked a bit gloomy so she knew Caroline hadn't showed up. But Lizzie had other things on her mind apart from Tom's love life. Was what Griffo said really true? And if it was, why hadn't the grown ups said anything about it? And why did all the books pretend that farms were lovely jolly places where the hens all scratched around amongst the grass and stones and laid their eggs in the barn? Lizzie felt excited and a bit angry, too.

She had a boiled egg for her tea. There was nothing odd about it. It tasted just like boiled eggs always did. A bit of yolk ran down her chin, which annoyed her rather, especially as it gave Tom a chance to tease.

"Hey, Mum! Fetch Lizzie's old bibs out!" he said. "Ha ha! The yolk's on you, Lizzie!"

"Oh, that boy," said Kalamazoo, who was lying face down on the sofa having one of his headaches. "These jokes...*jokes*? We cannot call them that. They are the outpourings of an inferior mind."

After she had wiped her chin, Lizzie turned her egg shell upside down and drew a face on it. Somehow the face turned out angry, with a terrific frown.

"Mum..." said Lizzie, "you know Dewey's? Is it really an egg farm?"

"Well, of course it is, Lizzie," said Mrs Green from behind a mountain of labels. "You can read, can't you? It says so on the gate." Lizzie's mum was a bit bad-tempered this evening. She looked pale.

"But, Mum," Lizzie went on, "do the hens really all live in boxes and never come out or anything?"

"I don't know, love. I suppose so."

"But that's horrible!"

Mrs Green licked another envelope.

"Well, I can't do anything about it, Lizzie," she sighed. "Clear away and do the washing up, will you, please love?"

"And Tom! He's got to help!"

Tom was lying on the sofa watching American football with his dad.

"Tom! Come and help with the washing-up!" called Mrs Green half-heartedly.

"In a minute!" grumbled Tom, still staring at the screen.

"Mum...?"

"Oh, what is it now?"

"You know Paul Griffin?"

"Who?...Oh, yes."

"He says he'll take me and Tom round Dewey's if we want to. He works there."

"Oh. Very nice, love."

"Is it all right, then? All right if I go?"

"What – Yes! Don't bother me now, Lizzie. I'm trying to concentrate on these addresses."

Slowly Lizzie cleared away the supper and stacked the dirty dishes by the sink. She knew there was no point in asking Tom to help until the American football was finished, so she wandered out to the garden with Kalamazoo. It wasn't much of a garden. Lizzie's dad wasn't interested in gardening, and her mum never had enough time for it, so there was just a sort of wilderness of long grass and weeds. Lizzie liked to sit out there, on the back step, and bite the juicy ends off the grass stalks. It always helped her to think.

"We could hide in that long grass," said Kalamazoo. "Instead of going to Dewey's tomorrow morning. Nobody would ever find us."

Lizzie was feeling a little nervous, too. But she didn't want Kalamazoo to know it. If he did, he'd go right off the deep end.

"Still," he mused. "I suppose there might be snakes in the grass. Maybe we should just stay indoors. It's probably safer. Are you sure that grass is all right to chew? You're not going to choke or anything, I hope."

"Honestly, Kalamazoo!" said Lizzie, laughing. "You act like my mum, sometimes."

In fact, she thought rather sadly, Mum doesn't seem to have time to fuss over me any more, what with all this work she has to do. So maybe it's nice having a Bear who's a nervous wreck, worrying about me all the time.

"We're going to Dewey's, Kalamazoo," she said. "And we're going tomorrow. There's nothing to be frightened of."

But deep down, in her heart of hearts, she wasn't all that sure.

4

Into the Unknown

"There he is," said Tom. Griffo was sitting on his bike by the entrance to Dewey's Eggs. Lizzie felt excited. She had managed to get Tom and Kalamazoo to come with her, otherwise she might have been too scared to turn up. Kalamazoo was shaking slightly, but pretending to perfectly relaxed.

"It's a n-n-nice day for it," he whispered into Lizzie's sweatshirt.

"He's not really mad, is he, Tom?" asked Lizzie very quietly as they walked towards

Griffo.

"As a hatter," said Tom with a wicked grin.

They followed Griffo up the drive. It was a Sunday, so there was nobody there. It was Griffo's job to come in on Sundays and feed the hens, and make sure everything was all right. He propped his bike against the wall and got out a big bunch of keys. *It's like going into a prison,* thought Lizzie. *They're all locked in.* And the thought of it made her shudder even though the day was warm.

The door swung open, and they stepped inside. It was dark, and there was a terrible smell, and an awful sound – hundreds of hens groaning in their cages. The smell and the noise almost suffocated Lizzie. She felt sick, she felt dizzy, and she only just managed to stay there without running away. At first she couldn't see anything, but then, gradually, her eyes got used to the dark

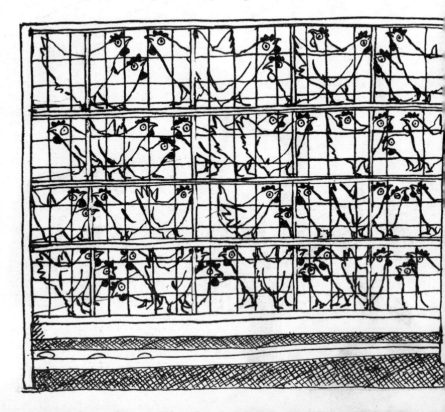

and she could make out rows and rows of cages. They were tiny little boxes, no bigger than a TV set. And in each box several hens were crammed – four or five to a box – so that they couldn't even move. They grumbled and pecked at one another, and fluttered helplessly with scrawny, half-bald wings and all the time the sickening smell seemed to get stronger and stronger.

"I'm going to faint," whispered Kalamazoo. Lizzie held him tight, but a wave of panic came over her. She wanted to get out.

"I—I'm..." she faltered.

Griffo leered at her with a nasty tormenting smile.

"What's the matter?" he asked, showing his yellow teeth. "You chicken? Har har!"

Lizzie recovered. She wasn't going to let her feelings show.

"It's nothing," she said. "I'm not sure if I left my watch at home, that's all."

Tom was walking down the line of cages.

"Look," he said. "Their feed is on a conveyor belt, sort of thing."

"Yeah," said Griffo. "I've got to put some more tranquilliser into it. We like to keep 'em nice and dopey. Less trouble."

Lizzie noticed that under the cages, the droppings were piling up on the floor. She wondered when they got cleaned out. It seemed awful that creatures should have to live like that. For a minute she felt very sick again, but she pulled herself together.

"How long do hens live?" she asked.

"They don't last long," said Griffo. "Not these 'uns, anyway. They're burnt out after seven or eight months. Lay themselves to death." Lizzie hardly dared ask the next question.

"What...what happens to them then?"

"Sold for meat," said Griffo. "It's part of my job to spot the ones that are finished. See that 'un there?" He pointed to a cage next to Lizzie's elbow. "She's had it, that one. She'll be on somebody's dinner table by next Sunday."

And he moved on to where Tom was fiddling with one of the machines.

Lizzie looked into the cage where the condemned hen was. She had a sad look about her, as if she had heard and understood what Griffo said. Her feathers were patchy and there were scabs on her body. A little frill of white feathers around her neck made her look as if she was wearing a scarf. For a moment Lizzie stared into the cage and the hen peered back, right into her eyes. It made a soft crooning sound as if to say hello.

"Hello," whispered Lizzie. "You poor old thing."

"Buck buck-buck ba-duuuuck!" answered the hen.

"We'll rescue you," said Lizzie. "Won't we, Kalamazoo?"

"You leave me out of it," said Kalamazoo. "The situation is appalling, sure, but what can we do? I don't want to get on the wrong side of that person with the teeth."

Lizzie glanced down the shed to where Griffo and Tom were looking into a kind of office. They were quite far away.

"Quick, Kalamazoo," she hissed. "I'm going to unzip you!"

"What?" said Kalamazoo. "Here? For goodness' sake – "

But before he had time to argue, Lizzie had unzipped him. Then she opened the hen's cage, and very gently reached in and lifted her out. The hen let herself be lifted. She looked puzzled but she seemed to recognise, by the careful way Lizzie held her, that she was a friend. Then came the tricky part. Very carefully, and whispering comforting things to the hen all the time, Lizzie placed her inside Kalamazoo's tummy and did up the zip.

The chicken flapped a bit, but then seemed

to get used to the idea and was still. But Kalamazoo was outraged.

"Take this chicken out of my tummy, this minute!" he cried. "How dare you? You know I don't like chicken! I'm a vegetarian! This is awful! Its claws are scratching me! Its feathers are tickling me!"

And despite himself, Kalamazoo began to laugh, hysterically, because of the tickling.

"You must be brave, Kalamazoo," said Lizzie. "It's only for a very short while – till we get home."

Then she called out to Tom and Griffo, who were down at the other end of the building.

"I'm going home now! I've seen enough! And I don't want to miss *Blue Peter* on telly!"

And before they could answer, she ran out of the building, clutching Kalamazoo firmly under her arm.

All the way home, Kalamazoo's belly flapped and went *buck buck-buck ba-duck*. And all the way home Kalamazoo moaned and complained.

"What will people think?" he cried. "Look at my tummy! It's galloping about! It's completely out of control!"

"Well, if anybody asks," said Lizzie, "we can tell them that you've got galloping gutrot. That you ate something that's disagreeing with you."

"I hope you realise just how heroic this all is!" said Kalamazoo. "It's not many people who've smuggled out prisoners in their own insides!"

"Yes, yes!" said Lizzie. "You'll get a medal!"

Soon they were home. Lizzie's mum and dad were busy painting the bathroom, so it was easy for Lizzie to smuggle the hen through the house and out into the back garden. There she unzipped Kalamazoo and let the hen out. She sat there stunned, blinking in the daylight, then made a weak fluttering movement and fell onto her side. She couldn't walk. Being cooped up in that cage all her life, she had either forgotten how to, or was too weak.

"I hope she'll be all right!" she whispered.

"Never mind her!" said Kalamazoo. "What about me? Zip me up! All this sunshine is terribly bad for my innards! I wouldn't be surprised if I got an ulcer."

5

Fight the Good Fight

There was chicken for lunch, but somehow Lizzie couldn't face it. She ate the potatoes and beans, but she couldn't forget the look in the eyes of her hen, and it made eating chicken impossible.

"I hope you're not going to go all cranky on us, Lizzie," said her mum. "If I'd known the trip round Dewey's would have this effect on you, I'd never have let you go."

"But Mum!" said Lizzie, "it's so horrible!

The poor hens are locked away all day and all night! And their droppings just pile up underneath them! It smells awful! And the hens all look terrible!"

"It's not my fault, Lizzie," said her mum, looking rather flustered.

"Why do they do it, Dad?" asked Lizzie. "Why are they allowed to do it? Why can't hens run about in the open air like they used to?"

"Well," said Dad, picking his teeth with slow deliberation, "some do. There are places where the hens can run about. Free Range, it's called."

"Why don't we buy free range eggs then, Mum?" asked Lizzie. "Please!"

"They're too expensive, love," said her mum, looking a bit uneasy.

"It's economics, see, Lizzie," said her dad. "The man who owns the hens, see, it costs him less to run the place. So he makes more money."

"That's right," said Mum. "If the hens run all over the place, he'd have to pay lots of people to look after them. And it would take  them ages to find the eggs, wouldn't it?"

Lizzie didn't like the sound of economics. She helped her mum to clear away and wash up, but she didn't talk much. She was busy thinking. Her mum noticed how silent she was, and tried to distract her.

"How are you getting on with your skates fund, love?" she asked. "You must've saved quite a bit by now."

Lizzie had. She got fifty pence pocket money every week, and she always saved most of it.

Then, suddenly, Lizzie had a brain wave. That was the answer! She could donate some of her pocket money to buy the free range eggs.

"Mum!" she said. "If I give up forty pence of my pocket money every week, could you use that to buy free range eggs? Oh please, Mum! Please!" Lizzie's mum put down the tea towel. She looked very hard for a moment. Then she gave her a hug.

"You're really steamed up about this free range business, aren't you, love?" she said. "All right, it's a deal. If you're prepared to give up your pocket money for what you believe in, good luck to you."

"Oh, thank you, Mum! Thanks ever so!"

Lizzie gave her mum a hug and a kiss. Then she ran out to the garden.

She had another problem to solve. Was the hen still there? And if she was, what would her parents say when they found out? Lizzie made a soft clucking noise, and down at the bottom of the garden, the long grass moved.

"Gwen!" called Lizzie. She had decided that the hen was called Gwen. It seemed to suit her. It was a henny sort of name. "Gwen!" The grass rustled, and Gwen peeped out cautiously from behind a dock leaf.

Lizzie walked slowly down to where Gwen was. And there, in a sort of snug little hollow she had made for herself in the grass, was a brown egg. Lizzie was delighted. Gwen looked up shyly at her, as if to say: *here's a thank you present for rescuing me.* Lizzie picked the egg up. It was still warm.

"Oh, thank you, Gwen!" said Lizzie. "See? You're not finished after all. Do you like this garden? Would you like to live here?"

"Lizzie!" came her mother's voice from the back door. "Who are you talking to? What's that? A hen? Where on earth did that come from? What's going on?"

Lizzie told her mum the whole story about how she had rescued Gwen, and how if she hadn't, Gwen would've ended up on someone's dinner table.

"I want to keep her as a pet," said Lizzie. "Oh, please, Mum! Nobody else wants her."

Mum thought for a minute.

"The trouble is, Lizzie," she explained, "the hen doesn't belong to us. It belongs to Mr Dewey. You may have thought you were rescuing her, but in Mr Dewey's eyes, you were stealing her."

"But he'd finished with her! Griffo said so."

"Well, then he'd have sold her for meat."

"Wait!" said Lizzie, and ran upstairs to her bedroom. She grabbed her piggy bank and ran down again. She emptied the piggy bank on to the back step. There was five pounds in it.

"Will that be enough, Mum? Enough to buy Gwen? I don't mind paying for her as long as I can keep her and let her live here."

Lizzie's mum smiled a very odd sort of smile. She took a pound of Lizzie's money and gave the rest back to her.

"I'll write and explain to Mr Dewey," she said. "And I'll send him a cheque. I'm sure it'll be all right."

Lizzie thought for a minute.

"Mum..." she said, "if you're going to write to Mr Dewey, can I put a letter in with it? I want to ask him not to put his hens in cages any more."

Mum sighed, smiling.

"You never give up, do you, Lizzie? All right."

So Lizzie wrote her letter. She didn't get a reply. She still writes, though – every week.

One day, she says, Mr Dewey'll get fed up of all the letters and set the hens free. He'll certainly give up if nobody buys his eggs any more – if everybody buys free-range instead. Because, as Lizzie's dad says,

"It won't be economical then."

Gwen the hen seems very happy in Lizzie's back garden. Tom built a little house for her to go in at night. Gwen's feathers got thicker and thicker, and now they really shine. And she doesn't seem finished at all, in fact, every so often, she lays an egg for Lizzie's tea. Which means that Lizzie doesn't have to give up quite so much of her pocket

money for the free range eggs. After all, she's got a free range hen of her very own—living in her back garden.

"We'll win one day, Kalamazoo," says Lizzie. "One day there won't be any more hens in prison. They'll all be able to scratch round in the sunshine. Yes! We'll win!"

"Don't bring me into it," moans Kalamazoo. "I still haven't recovered from that last adventure of yours. Just don't let's talk about Dewey's Eggs – I can't even bear to think about it."

"But we've got to think about it!" says Lizzie. "Or we can't do anything about it! Can we?"

What do *you* think?